libraries ni

You can renew your book at any library or online at
www.librariesni.org.uk

If you require help please email - enquiries@librariesni.org.uk

Ring of Roses

MARY HOOPER

Barrington Stoke

First published in 2014 in Great Britain by
Barrington Stoke Ltd
18 Walker Street, Edinburgh, EH3 7LP

www.barringtonstoke.co.uk

A CIP catalogue record for this book is available
from the British Library upon request

ISBN: 978-1-78112-401-7

Printed in China by Leo

 For Mackenzie and Nate

 CHAPTER I

The great house buzzed with noise and activity. The cook pummelled bread dough in the kitchen. The housekeeper hummed as she folded bed linen. The upstairs maids and downstairs maids came and went with buckets of coal or chamber pots. The kitchen maid sang as she scrubbed the doorstep.

Mrs Beauchurch spoke with Abigail in the best bedchamber. This was a splendid room with hand-painted wallpaper, crystal mirrors and paintings of the Beauchurch family through the ages. Among the pieces of shiny polished furniture, there were two huge wardrobes and a four-poster bed with velvet drapes. There was also a carved wooden rocking cradle.

Abby looked into the cradle, but the baby inside was bundled up and not much could be seen of her. She was awake, however, and her eyes were big and blue with dark lashes all round. Abby gazed at her, and fell in love at first sight.

"This is Grace," Mrs Beauchurch said.

"What a beautiful child!" Abby said. She put out a hand to rock the cradle and remembered her manners. "*Very* beautiful – if I might say so, Madam."

Mrs Beauchurch gave a weak smile. "Of course you may. But weren't your sisters beautiful when they were babies?"

Abby shook her head. "They had screwed up faces, or were scrawny, or always screaming. But little Grace here ... I do believe I never saw a prettier or more contented babe in all my life."

"Well, we are in agreement about that," Mrs Beauchurch said, and sank back onto her feather pillows and linen sheets.

It was rather strange, Abby thought, to have an interview with an employer who was in bed.

But Mrs Beauchurch explained that the long labour and birth of Grace had left her worn out. "I *had* wanted to look after Grace by myself," she told Abby, "but it's as much as I can do to get out of bed by noon – and that's with the help of two maids. I need a nursemaid."

Abby did not reply for a moment. She was gazing round in wonder at the furnishings of the room, at the sparkling mirrors, thick, soft rugs and jewel-coloured hangings. She had never seen such a room in all her life.

With an effort, Abby tried to concentrate on what Mrs Beauchurch was saying. "You shouldn't rush things, Madam," she said. "My mother always takes at least two months to get back on her feet after a little one comes."

Mrs Beauchurch nodded. "Are you called Abigail or Abby?"

"Abby, Madam."

"Well, Abby, I want someone who will give little Grace as much tender love and care as I would."

Abby glanced over at the baby and smiled. "Have no fears on that, Madam!"

Mrs Beauchurch gave Abby a keen look before she spoke again. "You'll answer to Mrs Dimmock the cook, and Mrs Bailey the housekeeper," she said. "You will be in charge of all Grace's wants and needs. It will be your job to play with her, wash her clothes, blankets and bedding, and keep her safe and happy. She must want for nothing."

Abby nodded. "And what about her feeding, Madam?" she asked. Abby knew from experience that this was more important than anything else.

"A wet nurse calls in four times a day," Mrs Beauchurch said.

Abby nodded again. "Very good, Madam."

"Mrs Tomkins is a clean and respectable woman with a baby of her own," Mrs Beauchurch went on.

Abby smiled.

"I know that babies pick up sickness easily," Mrs Beauchurch said. "I don't want Grace to be taken into public places."

"No, Madam," Abby said.

"If you go to market, or run errands, she must stay home in the care of Mrs Bailey or Mrs Dimmock." Mrs Beauchurch paused, then asked, "And where was your last position, Abby?"

"In Kensington," Abby replied proudly. "I had two little girls to care for – the granddaughters of a lord. I looked after them for a year, but then their father said they must have a governess and learn languages."

"I don't think Grace will be ready for that for a while," Mrs Beauchurch said, with a little smile. "But how many sisters did you say you had?"

"Six, Madam," Abby said. "All younger than me."

"Then there are *seven* of you?"

Abby nodded. "Seven so far. Me – Abigail – then Bess, Clara, Dora ..."

Mrs Beauchurch raised a hand for her to stop. Enough!" she said, but her voice was kind. "The idea of having seven little girls makes me feel quite weak. How far does your mother intend to go through the alphabet?"

"I think she will go on until she has a boy," Abby said, and Mrs Beauchurch shook her head in disbelief.

There was a moment's silence while both of them gazed at the baby. Then Mrs Beauchurch said, "I believe you will suit us very well, Abby." She gave her another keen look. "I have waited six long years for Grace and feel that she will be my only child. Do you promise to love and cherish her? Would you put her life before your own?"

"Indeed I would, Madam," Abby vowed.

"Then you may start here tomorrow," said Mrs Beauchurch. "I'll ask Mrs Bailey the housekeeper to have a bed put up in the nursery for you." Then she closed her eyes to signal that the interview was at an end.

Abby dropped into a curtsey (despite the fact Mrs Beauchurch couldn't see her) and left the room.

Belle Vue House was a large Tudor building in the centre of London, with its own barn, stables and carriages. The Beauchurches were just a family of three, but they had a large number of indoor and outdoor servants.

"Rather you than me, caring for *that* precious babe," Lizzie the kitchen maid said when she met Abby the next day. "Infants go down with every sniffle and sickness known to man – and it always turns out to be their nursemaid's fault."

Abby laughed. "I looked after all my sisters as babes and never lost a single one!"

"Besides, there are rumours ..." Lizzie said darkly.

"What sort of rumours?" Abby asked.

"About – you know." Lizzie dropped her voice. "*The Plague.* They say it has started up again. There have been signs in the sky."

"*In the sky?*" Abby repeated. "How can that be?"

"They say an angel appeared in the clouds with a flaming sword," Lizzie said. "And a comet with a tail of fire shot across the sky."

Abby considered this. "But have many people actually *caught* the Plague?" she asked. 'Was this why Mrs Beauchurch didn't want Grace to be taken into public places?' she wondered.

Lizzie shrugged. "Don't know – although rumour has it that the richest families are already leaving London for their country homes."

"But the King is still here in Whitehall, is he not?" Abby said.

Lizzie nodded. "When *he* goes from London, that will be the time to worry."

The cook, Mrs Dimmock, came into the kitchen and clapped her hands at the sight of the two girls chatting. "Lizzie, gossiping again!" she scolded. "I never saw a more idle girl in my life!" Mrs Dimmock frowned at Abby. "I hope you're not going to take after her."

"No, Mrs Dimmock," Abby said.

"Lizzie – clear the ashes out of the grates downstairs and polish them," Mrs Dimmock ordered. "Abby, you can go and make up your bed in the nursery. And use the back stairs, of course."

Abby was about to set off when the cook added, "One baby won't be a lot of work. When you're at a loose end, come to me and I'll find you something to do. There's knives to polish, for a start. And there's 102 of them."

"Yes, Mrs Dimmock," Abby said, and made up her mind that she'd always try to look busy.

Abby had reached the door to the back stairs when two boys about her own age burst in. One had dark hair, and one was fair. The fair one looked perfectly pleasant, but the dark one was so *very* handsome that Abby felt herself blush just looking at him. They were dressed in dark blue uniforms and had a pleasant smell of leather and horses about them.

"Mrs Dimmock!" the fair one said, breathless. "There's a house shut up in Old Street!"

"Next to the church!" the dark one said.

"Planks over the windows and door …"

"… with a big red cross on it that says 'LORD HAVE MERCY ON US'."

The cook sat down with a thud. "Gawd help us," she said. "The rumours must be true …"

"We ran past the house as fast as we could!" the dark boy said.

"They say if you as much as breathe the air from a tainted house you'll die," the fair one added.

"Stuff and nonsense," Mrs Dimmock said, but she didn't sound sure.

"Shall we go into the yard and get some snails?" the dark one asked.

"Whatever for?" Lizzie asked.

"They say that if you keep 12 snails in your mouth when you go out, it's a sure guard against the Plague," the fair-haired one told her.

"More stuff and nonsense," Mrs Dimmock said.

" 'Tis hot enough for Plague," the dark-haired youth said. Then he noticed Abby and stopped and smiled. "Hello," he said. "My name's Toby."

His fair-haired friend shoved him out of the way. "Never mind him – I'm James," he said.

Abby smiled and nodded to each of them in turn. Working here was going to be even better than she'd hoped.

Abby's days fell into a pattern. Little Grace woke about five o'clock every morning, and it was Abby's job to keep her quiet until the wet nurse arrived at seven. Most mornings she would take Grace downstairs. If the day was fair, she would tuck the baby into the cradle, which swung from the apple tree in the yard. Sometimes, with a little rocking, Grace would fall asleep again. Other times, Abby would carry her round the yard, in and out of the stables, and sing to her to try and keep her from waking Mr and Mrs Beauchurch.

Toby and James slept in the big hayloft above the stables. Sometimes Toby would hear Abby singing to Grace in the mornings and get up to keep her company. In this way, they became good friends.

CHAPTER 2

One morning, Grace had been fed and Abby was on her usual morning mission to fetch water from the well in Bell Court. This was a pleasant square near the busy jumble of lanes around Belle Vue House.

The well at Bell Court was a popular place, for the water there came from a spring outside the city, not the polluted and smelly River Thames. As well as the long line of cooks and maids who were always at the well, there were three or four market stalls and a dozen or so peddlers, who hoped to sell things to those who were waiting their turn.

Abby joined the line of maids with jugs and pails, and she had almost reached the well, when her eye was caught by a girl who'd just arrived.

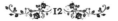

That red hair, those freckles – she looked just like a girl from Abby's home village.

"Hannah?" Abby called, and the girl turned, surprised. "Hannah!" Abby waved and called again. "It's me, Abby!"

A smile spread across Hannah's face. "Abigail Palmer! Whatever are you doing here?"

Abby laughed, then left her place in the line and went to hug Hannah. "The same as you," she said. "Waiting to draw up water."

"But you look so very smart!" Hannah said, and stood back to admire Abby's uniform of dark cotton gown and white apron trimmed with lace. "Where are you living?"

Abby pointed across Bell Court. "In Belle Vue House – near the river. I work for the Beauchurch family."

"Do they not have a well of their own?" Hannah asked in surprise.

Abby nodded. "But 'tis more fun to come here and gossip with the other girls!"

"And are you a maid-servant?"

"A nursemaid," Abby answered, "with one baby in my charge – Grace Emilia Beauchurch. The sweetest child you ever saw."

"It is no surprise that you are a nursemaid!" Hannah said, for she knew of Abby's big family.

Abby nodded and laughed. "As soon as I said that I had six little sisters, the job was mine."

"And do you like living in London?" Hannah asked.

"Of course!" Abby looked at the people around them – a mix of peddlers selling ribbons, hair combs, rat traps, oranges and push-along toys, rich folk passing by in silks and velvets, and the poor in rags. "There are new things to look at every day," she said.

" 'Tis true!" Hannah laughed.

"Why, you can get a tooth pulled or watch a flea circus, eat sweetmeats or buy a puppy here, all before noon."

"That is what my sister and I are selling," Hannah said.

"Puppies?" Abby asked.

Hannah laughed. "No! Sweetmeats. We make frosted rose petals, marzipan fruits, sugared rosemary and the like," she said. "Our shop is at the Sign of the Sugared Plum in Crown and King Place."

"Then I shall come and find you!" Abby linked her arm through Hannah's. "Now, tell me the gossip from home, for I have not heard a thing from my ma or sisters."

Hannah was about to say that was because nothing ever happened at home, when both girls noticed a poster on the wall nearby. This bore the word 'PLAGUE' in large letters. "Plague – the most damnable of diseases!" Hannah read out loud.

Abby shivered, for all the day was hot. Both girls had learned to read at the same Dame School, and now Abby carried on reading over Hannah's shoulder: "A sure prev-ent-ative for this most horrible pest-i-lence may be purchased from Dr Chomsky's Apoth-ecary Shop at the Sign of the Blue Ball."

The girls fell silent for a moment.

"Do you think it's true?" Hannah asked after a moment. "*Has* the Plague arrived?"

"They are saying so," Abby said. "It seems there's a house shut up in Church Street, though I haven't seen it for myself."

"I've heard about that," Hannah said in a hushed voice. "The mistress of the house passed away, and now her husband and children and servants have to be shut in until 40 days have gone by. But if one of *them* should have the bad fortune to die, then the 40 days start all over again."

"But I am sure it will not affect me or you," Abby said, "for we are from healthy country stock!"

"Indeed we are!" Hannah agreed.

As they went back to the line at the well, both girls resolved to put such worrying matters from their minds. "Now, tell me," Abby said. "Do you have a sweetheart?"

Hannah shook her head. "I do not. Do you?"

"At the house where I work there's a lad called Toby and he's *very* handsome," Abby told her. "We speak a lot when the cook, Mrs Dimmock, isn't around, and he makes me laugh and I think that ... yes, when the moment comes I shall let him kiss me!"

Hannah laughed. "I must find a sweetheart soon, for I have a great wish to go to the theatre and I have heard that it's not done for a girl to go there alone."

"Only whores do that!" Abby whispered in Hannah's ear, and both girls giggled at Abby's boldness in using such a word.

"The theatre is all very well," Abby said, "but have you ever been to the Royal Exchange?"

Hannah shook her head. "Never. What is it?"

" 'Tis where the big city men go to do business," Abby said. "But it's also where the rich folk meet and flirt with each other. You can buy scented gloves, buttons and bows or, if you wish, you can go into a coffee shop or take an iced drink."

"And do *you* do all those things?" Hannah asked.

Abby smiled and shook her head. "No. I have only been once before when I was at my previous job – as I said, 'tis for lords and ladies and the rich. But there's nothing to stop us going to look at them."

"Then do let's!" Hannah said. "It will be easy to talk my sister into letting us go – but what about your mistress?"

"She is still lying-in after the birth," Abby said, "and she sleeps a lot of the time, so I could go when little Grace is asleep."

"Does the babe not go out with you?" Hannah asked.

Abby shook her head. "They have forbidden it because of the risk of illness. She's my mistress's only child and very precious."

"Does the poor child never see daylight, then?"

Abby laughed. "Yes, she has a cradle in the tree. But she doesn't go outside the yard, because they fear that some scrawny beggar might breathe his foul breath on her and pass on the ..." But Abby didn't want to use the word in case it was bad luck. "Let's go to the Exchange next week!" she said instead.

# CHAPTER 3

THE FIRST WEEK OF JULY, 1665

The weather grew hotter and people said that they had never known a summer like it. Dogs died for the want of puddle-water to drink, vegetables shrivelled in the fields and people fainted in the streets. As the heat increased degree by degree, so did the number of Plague victims.

At the start of July near 500 people died in one week. It became harder to buy food, and shops began to close. Some of the owners had caught the Plague, some didn't want to risk serving the public, and some had moved away.

Desperate measures were called for and, in a bid to halt the spread of infection, the Justices paid a Frenchman to fumigate a number of houses in the city. He burned brimstone and

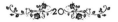

other things together – he swore that he'd already stopped the Plague in Paris that way. It caused a choking smoke, but it did nothing to stop the Plague. People began to say that the Plague was a punishment from God for His people, and only He could make it halt.

Abby and Hannah, however, still went on their planned outing to the Royal Exchange. They chattered all the way.

"This friend I have – Tom – is learning to be an apothecary and he makes all sorts of pills and potions to keep Plague away," Hannah said.

"But do they work?" Abby asked.

Hannah sighed. "That's just it, he doesn't know. His master says that no one knows what causes Plague – and no one knows what cures it, either."

"Mrs Dimmock says that Plague spreads fastest among the poor," Abby said. "Those who live higgledy-piggledy ten to a room."

"I've been told it doesn't care where it ends up," Hannah said. "The King could catch it as easily as you or I."

"I've heard that all cats and dogs are to be killed in case they are the ones who are spreading it," Abby said.

"I heard that too!" Hannah shook her head. "They'll pay four pence for every dead dog, and tuppence for a cat."

Both girls sighed, but as they neared the Royal Exchange, their spirits rose and their chatter turned to more pleasant topics like the newest colours for ribbons and the latest fashions from Paris. They were young and on such a jolly outing, and that made thoughts of death very easy to dismiss.

The Exchange was a large building with columns around its sides and an open area in the middle. In this space, people paraded – the women wore the latest in wigs, hats and silk and satin gowns and the men were dressed in the same showy materials and colours, with wigs that were primped and curled.

The shops inside the Exchange were small and candlelit. Their windows were prettily dressed to show off whatever it was they dealt in – crystallised fruits or scented gloves, nosegays or necklaces. Abby and Hannah looked around in wonder, for every shop was like a small treasure chest. Even the peddlers allowed in the Exchange were of a different class. They didn't sell rat traps or foot powder, but gold and silver ribbons, pomanders studded with cloves and sparkling hair combs.

"It's a most excellent place," said Hannah, who seemed not to know what to look at first. "I must tell my sister about it!"

"Yes," Abby said, with a small frown. "But it doesn't seem quite as lively as when I came before."

Hannah hesitated. "Do you think it's because of the ...?"

"Perhaps ..."

As they stopped to look in the window of a shop that sold scented candles, a well-dressed fellow came out and shook his head.

"Our information was correct," he said to another young fop. "The shop owner saw him with his own eyes."

"Never!" the other young man said.

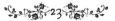

" 'Tis true, I tell you," the first said. "True as the Earth is round!"

Abby and Hannah exchanged glances. What had happened?

"Excuse me, Sir," Abby said boldly, to the one who'd spoken first. "What is it that's true?"

"He's gone!" came the reply. "Abandoned us."

"Who has?" Hannah asked.

"The King!" the man cried. "He was seen this morning, riding towards Hampton Court with a party of gentlemen. The word is that the Queen and Court will follow him, and they'll stay there, out of London, until the Plague is over."

"Then ... then it has truly started?" Abby asked, and shivered.

"1,000 dead this week alone," the second young man said. "They're trying to pretend they're not *all* from Plague, but they are. And the last deaths were pretty near the King's palace. That's why he's gone from London."

"If the rest of us have got any sense, we'll follow him!" the first fellow said.

"If only we can get a travel warrant," his friend added, and they rushed off.

Abby and Hannah, alarmed, looked at each other. All of a sudden, the day did not seem quite so fine, nor the Exchange such a box of delights.

CHAPTER 4

Abby looked around Dr Chomsky's shop. It was dark and musty, with bunches of dried bracken hanging from the beams and dead nettles and herbs all along the shelves. The only brightness came from strange bottles of red, purple and blue liquid that stood in the window.

The bell jangled as the door closed, and a strange creature came out from the back of the shop. "Well, young Miss, what can I do for you?" it asked, in a muffled voice.

Abby shrank back a little, for the creature had the head of a bird, and its great black cloak folded round its body like wings. "Are ... are you Dr Chomsky the apothecary?" she asked.

"I am," the creature said.

"I saw your poster in Bell Court," Abby said. "I'd like to purchase some of your mixture to prevent Plague, please."

"Very wise." Dr Chomsky's eyes glittered behind the mask. "Have you 20 shillings?"

"20 shillings!" Abby gasped. "No! I ... I hadn't thought that it would be so costly."

"No? When 20 years of skill and knowledge have gone into its brewing?"

"Why, 'tis more than I can earn in a year!" Abby cried.

"Ah." Dr Chomsky waved towards the door. "It seems, then, that Dr Chomsky's mixture is not for you."

"No, it doesn't seem as if it is." Abby wondered if she could make the mixture herself, and so she asked, "But will you tell me what it contains?"

"Indeed I will not!" the doctor said. "I mix it by moonlight with certain secret and rare plants known only to myself."

Abby hadn't held out much hope that he *would* tell her ... but there was something else she wanted to know. "Will you tell me, instead, why you wear that bird's head?" she asked. "Is it to frighten people so that they buy from you?"

Dr Chomsky hesitated a moment and then removed the strange head. Abby was left looking at an ordinary middle-aged man.

"No, not for that reason," Dr Chomsky said. "It is just what an apothecary wears when he goes to treat those who have the sickness." He tipped up the bird's head to show her the inside of it. "See here, it is but a mask stuffed with herbs. When I breathe in, my breath comes through the herbs and is cleansed."

"Then perhaps everyone should be given a bird's head to wear!" Abby said.

"Perhaps they should," said Dr Chomsky. He sighed. "But I don't believe that anything will stop the Plague now."

"Not even your mixture?" Abby asked.

Dr Chomsky shook his head. "The King and his Court have gone from London and all of the rich will follow them. There will be no one left who can afford to buy from me anyway."

Abby tried to feel sorry for him but could not. "So, is there *nothing* anyone can do to help themselves?" she asked. "Nothing that will stop it at all?"

"They do say that if you hold 12 snails in your mouth when you –"

"No!" Abby said. "I have heard that and will not do it."

"If you can obtain a dead man's skull, you should scrape off the moss and –"

"No!" Abby said again. "Not that."

"Then your only hope is to get out of the city as fast as you can." The doctor turned the sign on his door to say 'CLOSED'. "That's what I'm doing."

Abby was very thoughtful as she started back towards Belle Vue House. She wanted to save time, for Mrs Tomkins would soon be arriving to feed Grace, and so she took a shortcut through St Giles, the poorest parish in London. Here she was shocked to see three houses in a row shut up, all with red crosses painted on their doors.

She stopped in horror at the end of the road. How many people were shut inside? Someone was screaming in one of the attic rooms and a woman's pitiful voice called, "My child! Oh, my baby!"

Abby's eyes filled with tears. She knew she wouldn't be able to bear it if anything happened to Grace.

Back at the nursery in Belle Vue House, Abby got a small glass of beer ready for Mrs Tomkins and plumped up a cushion for her in a comfortable chair. She went into the yard to collect Grace from her cradle, then laid a blanket on the ground. She undid the baby's blankets and let her have a few moments of freedom. Grace kicked her legs and waved her arms. When Abby wrapped her up again, she checked each pink and plump baby limb and said a prayer that they

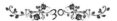

should stay that way. She would rather have the sickness herself than Grace should have it.

Grace was very hungry by then, and Abby carried her as far as the gate so that she could look down the lane and see if Mrs Tomkins was coming. Five minutes went by, then ten and 15, and it got harder and harder to soothe the baby. It was half past the hour when Abby left a screaming Grace with Mrs Dimmock and went to ask Mrs Beauchurch what she should do.

Mrs Beauchurch was very much alarmed. She told Abby to run to the nearest dairy and to ask the cow-keeper to send a cow and dairy maid – whatever it cost – to the house right away. "They must come three times a day from now on," she said. "If we cannot rely on Mrs Tomkins then we must find other means." She was very pale, Abby noticed, and her hands trembled on the satin bedcover as she spoke. "Tell the cow-keeper there will be a bonus if they maintain regular hours."

"Yes, Madam." Abby bobbed a curtsey, then said, "Excuse me, Madam, but they do say ass's milk is easier for a baby to digest than milk from a cow."

"Then we will have a milk-ass call!" Mrs Beauchurch declared. Her hands clutched at the bedcovers. "But how will my darling take the milk?"

Abby smiled to reassure her. "Once – I believe it was with Dora – my mother didn't have enough milk. She showed me how to trickle ass's milk down my fingers and into the baby's mouth."

"Indeed." Mrs Beauchurch laid back again in relief. "I bless the day you came to the house, Abby, for I know you have my child's best interests at the heart of everything you do."

CHAPTER 5

THE THIRD WEEK OF JULY, 1665

No one at Belle Vue House ever saw Mrs Tomkins again. Mrs Dimmock sent Abby to try and discover what had happened to her, but Abby found her rooms empty. Perhaps she had the Plague and she had been forced to go into a pest house. Either that, or she'd managed to travel out of London.

This would have been difficult, for guards had been posted at the big London gateways. No one could come in or out of the City without written permission – and that was not easy to get. It didn't stop the rich or the powerful, of course, for they could buy their way out, and they were followed by dozens of doctors who wanted to accompany their wealthy clients. The Beauchurches' own doctor went into the safety of the countryside. He left Belle Vue House with nothing but an expensive jug of treacle and a crock of rose jam as protection from the Plague.

The doctors who didn't leave were as likely to catch the disease as the next man. By the end of July, there was hardly a doctor to be found in the City.

Food became even more scarce and people had to travel to find it. Country women no longer wanted to come to the London markets to sell their wares. Instead, they brought their baskets to the City walls and set up stalls there. They kept bowls of vinegar beside their stalls. As they were paid for their eggs, greens or gingerbread, they would drop the coins into the vinegar in order to disinfect them.

All this while, Grace thrived under Abby's care and became more aware of the world around her. She started smiling, and Abby spent long times dancing about, singing nursery rhymes and playing 'peek-a-boo' to try and make her laugh. Grace was a happy baby – the most contented in the world, Abby thought. But then, Grace didn't know what was going on in the City, outside the gates of Belle Vue House.

"So many people have died that the graveyards are full up," Toby told Abby one morning. "They can't take any more bodies."

Abby stared at him in horror. "Never! What will they do with all the dead now?"

"Well, when people die they'll be collected on the death cart and –"

"*Death cart?*" Abby broke in.

Toby nodded. "They say there's no longer any time for proper funerals – too many people are dying. They're going to collect up the bodies on carts and throw them into pits – hundreds of bodies at a time. There'll be no fancy words and no fuss."

"Oh, how awful!" Abby cried.

Toby nodded. " 'Tis most shocking, but there's no other way."

The two of them stared at each other and then Toby took a step towards Abby. Abby wondered afterwards if he'd been about to kiss her, but she never found out because Mrs Dimmock shouted at her from the kitchen.

"Enough of the chatter, Miss! The mistress is calling for you."

Abby gave Toby a small smile. "I'd better go."

"*Now!*" Mrs Dimmock shouted. "Don't you dare keep Mrs Beauchurch waiting."

❦

Abby tapped at Mrs Beauchurch's bedroom door and went in. The room, as usual, was dark and stifling hot, for the mistress wouldn't allow the windows to be opened for fear of Plague coming in with a winged insect. She even chose not to see Grace, for she felt it would be better for the child that way. Just in case …

Abby took one glance at Mrs Beauchurch, restless in the grand bed, and knew she was as poorly as ever. Her face was drawn, her eyes sunken and her legs twitched all the while as she spoke. She coughed often, and in the end she went into a fit of choking which lasted several moments.

After Abby had given her some water, Mrs Beauchurch's first question was about Grace.

"She remains very well, Madam," Abby told her. "Hale and hearty on her ass's milk."

"Then let us pray God it continues," Mrs Beauchurch said. "Then we can plan our escape from London."

Abby stared at her, very surprised.

"Mr Beauchurch has managed to buy travel warrants for the three of us – you, me and Grace," her employer explained. "We are to go out of London to the fresh air of the countryside and live with my sister."

"Oh!" Abby felt rather excited, for she knew Mrs Beauchurch's sister was a real lady, rich and titled. "And where does your sister live, Madam?"

"She lives in Dorsetshire," Mrs Beauchurch said. "On a country estate, far away from any hint of the Plague. She'll shelter us there until the sickness has quite gone from London, and then we can return."

"Is Dorsetshire a long way off?" Abby asked.

"A three-day journey. We'll stay at coaching inns along the way." Once Mrs Beauchurch had said this, she fell to coughing again.

Abby, alarmed, fetched a cough mixture and gave Mrs Beauchurch a small glass of it. After a while, the fit passed and Mrs Beauchurch seemed more at peace. But Abby saw that the poor woman was ash-white and very weak, and there were blots of blood on her pillow. Perhaps she would improve in the peace and clean air of the countryside.

"When is it we'll be going, Madam?" Abby asked.

"As soon as ever we can, Abby. In a day or so. As soon as I'm well enough to travel."

"Of course, Madam," Abby said, but her heart sank. As soon as she was well enough to travel! What hope was there of *that*?

<hr>

That evening there was a curfew in London. Healthy people were asked to stay in their homes between the hours of eight and ten o'clock so that those with Plague could leave their houses and take the air.

Abby knew it was morbid, but she couldn't stop herself from standing beside the nursery window and looking out. The three lanes that met beside the house were already almost empty of people and animals. But as eight o'clock drew near, they cleared still further until it seemed that London was empty, a ghost town. Some minutes passed, and then Abby heard the tip-tapping of sticks on the cobbles and a raggle-taggle line of about 20 people appeared. Some looked very ill, as if they could hardly drag themselves along. Others seemed fairly normal, but were wailing or sobbing. Some were on crutches, and one man was naked apart from a piece of rag around his waist. He was scratching at his flesh as he went along, leaving weals on his chest and upper arms.

Abby shuddered. She'd heard that the lists of that week's Plague dead would show that over 2,000 had died. Was there nothing anyone could do? Were they *all* destined to die?

CHAPTER 6

Dozens of houses had been shut up and more were being closed off every day. At the end of July, Mr Beauchurch gave a strict talk to the servants in which he said that none of them should go into an area where there were infected houses. He also ordered that they should avoid crowds and not go to public wells to draw up water.

"We must only use the well in the yard," Abby said to Hannah, who had come to call on her. "That's why you haven't seen me in Bell Court."

"I wondered where you were," Hannah said. She was careful not to say that she'd feared the worst and that was why she'd come to call.

Mrs Dimmock the cook and Mrs Bailey the housekeeper were both out, so Abby let Hannah peep into some of the fine downstairs rooms of Belle Vue House.

Hannah gasped aloud at the sight of the dining room. "Such furniture! Those wall hangings!" she said, as she stared round in delight. "The Beauchurch family must be as rich as kings."

Abby nodded. "I believe they are."

"Do they entertain guests?"

Abby shook her head. "They do nothing. He works all hours and my mistress can scarce rise from her bed."

"Poor woman …" Hannah said.

"She is so thin her legs can barely hold her!" Abby cried. "A sparrow couldn't stay alive on what she eats."

"It's not …" Hannah lowered her voice. "… *Plague* that she has, is it?"

"No, it can't be that," Abby said. "From what people say, Plague strikes and kills fast."

Abby showed Hannah the drawing room and the dairy of Belle Vue House, and then she took her upstairs to the nursery to admire the sleeping Grace. "And of all the things in the house, here's the most beautiful," she whispered.

Hannah laughed. "You're like a doting mama!"

"But she *is*," Abby said.

By the end of July, each parish had taken on Searchers of the Dead to investigate deaths suspected to be Plague deaths. These Searchers were usually two old women who arrived at a house where someone had died, examined the body, and decided whether or not that person had been felled by Plague.

"But they are corrupt old devils," Toby told Abby. "If you give them a silver shilling, they'll say the death was because of the Purples or the Bloody Flux."

"Why would they do that?" Abby asked.

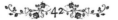

It was a warm evening and the two friends were in the yard of Belle Vue House. The full moon above them and the fruit-heavy apple tree made for a romantic setting, but the topic of conversation was not romantic in the least.

"If they say it's *not* Plague, the rest of the household don't have to be shut up for 40 days," Toby said.

"Oh. Of course."

There was a moment's silence before Toby went on. "I have been waiting to speak to you alone, Abby," he said.

"Have you?" Abby said. She wondered if he was going to ask her to walk out with him.

Toby nodded. "I wanted to let you know that James and I are planning to leave London and go into the country."

"Leave London?" Abby said in surprise. "But how can you do that without a warrant – without papers? I've heard there are guards at all the Gates and they watch the Bridge day and night."

"We've found a way to get across the Bridge in secret," Toby said. "We're going to wait until dark, then climb up on the back of a carriage and hitch a ride. We've been practising around the streets and we're quite good at it."

Abby sighed. "Then I shall miss you very much." She paused for a moment, and remembered her mistress's plans. "But perhaps I'll be going out of London, too," she said.

"Is Mrs Beauchurch better, then?" Toby asked. "Will she soon be well enough to travel?"

Abby thought about it for a moment, then sighed again. "To be honest, I think not. She was sick last night and has not risen from her bed for some days now. She gets weaker and weaker."

"Then come with us!" Toby begged her. "You can dress as a boy and jump up on the back of a carriage as well as we can. You said your home village was to the west – we'll help you find your way there."

Abby was silent, wondering if she could possibly do such a thing.

"I don't say this to frighten you," Toby said, "but they are saying that the sickness may go on until it destroys the City and everyone is dead."

Abby shivered. "Surely not. Surely it won't be that bad?"

"I fear it is." Toby took her hand. "What can you hear?"

Abby heard birdsong, the sound of running feet carrying a sedan chair and the noise of cart wheels on cobbles. But above all this was the constant toll of church bells, telling of some poor soul's passing.

"You hear those bells all the time now," Toby said. "There are funerals all day, every day of the week." He squeezed her hand. "Don't stay here and die, Abby. Come with us!"

Abby bit her lip. "I don't know ..."

How could she possibly leave Grace?

 # CHAPTER 7

THE FIRST WEEK OF AUGUST, 1665

"Repent! Repent!" the minister roared from the pulpit of St Stephen's Church. "Ask God's forgiveness for the dreadful sins you have committed, or suffer the Plague and die the most horrible death!"

As he spoke, Abby and the rest of the church-goers shifted in their seats, trying to think what they might have done to draw such a terrible punishment down on their heads.

The 2nd of August had been declared a day for fasting and prayer. Everyone in London was supposed to attend church at least once during that day. Some holy souls had already vowed that they would spend the whole day on their knees, praying that they would be spared. Abby sat at the back so as to be out of the eye of the

minister and listened, but she could not think
of any sins she needed to confess. She'd argued
with Lizzie and answered back to Mrs Dimmock,
but she was certain she'd done nothing that
might cause Plague.

" 'Tis not the people's fault. 'Tis all the King's
doing!" the man sitting in the pew next to Abby
said. "His Court is nothing but a den of vice and
sin, and God is showing his anger!"

Abby didn't reply. Mr Beauchurch had told
them that they were not to speak with strangers
for any reason.

"What example is our King setting to the rest
of us?" the man went on. "Why, he has three
mistresses, and he has children with all of them!
'Tis the King and his Court who are responsible
for this disaster, no one else!"

Abby moved a little further from the man,
then jumped as the minister thumped his open
Bible. "When you fall victim to this dread
disease – and you may be sure you will – nothing
awaits you but the fires of Hell!" he roared. "Fall
on your knees now and ask forgiveness for every
sin you have ever committed!"

He carried on in this vein for a whole hour, until Abby could not stand to hear any more and crept out of the church. She walked briskly back to Belle Vue House, trying to ignore the tolling of the church bells.

There were houses shut up everywhere she walked. In spite of Mr Beauchurch's orders it was impossible to avoid them all. The taverns and inns were closed too, and the theatres had signs outside to say that everything was cancelled until further notice. London seemed to be collapsing.

Abby sighed. Should she go with Toby? She'd still not given him a proper answer. Her first responsibility was Grace but, she reasoned, she was only the child's nursemaid. If she went out of London, then Mrs Beauchurch could find a replacement for her – couldn't she? But would that replacement love Grace as much as Abby did? It was not likely.

As Abby crossed what had been a busy market square just a few short weeks ago, she was alarmed to hear a harsh voice bellow, "Bring out your dead! Bring out your dead!"

The next moment, a farm cart came into view. Two men sat in the front seat, with their cloaks pulled around them, and their hoods pulled over their faces. One was ringing a hand-bell.

Abby gasped. She'd heard about the death carts, but she had never seen one before. Usually the collection and burial of bodies took place at night, under cover of darkness. Now, however, it appeared that the night hours did not provide enough time to collect all the bodies, and the carts had to go about their business during the day.

The cart stopped outside a small, plain house with the now common red cross on the door. 'LORD HAVE MERCY' was written in chalk on the brick walls. The door opened and Abby saw a body in the hallway. One of the men jumped down from the cart with a long sheep-hook in his hand. He fixed the hook around the body, and rolled it onto a sheet on the pavement. The other man opened the back of the cart, each of the men grabbed an end of the sheet, and they tossed the corpse up onto the cart. From where Abby was standing, she could see ten or 12 bodies already piled inside. They had been cast in higgledy-piggledy, some in winding sheets, some naked. All very much dead.

A sob caught in Abby's throat. They were all someone's wife, someone's husband, someone's children, she thought with horror, and now they were jumbled in together without respect or regard. All of a sudden she thought of Hannah. Abby hadn't seen her for some time now – was she all right? Abby must go to Crown and King Place and find out as soon as she could.

CHAPTER 8

The next afternoon, while Abby waited for the milk-ass to arrive, she went into the kitchens of Belle Vue House. There she found several of the servants standing around staring at Mrs Dimmock, who was hunched over in a chair, sobbing.

"She can't catch her breath to speak," Lizzie whispered to Abby. "All we know is that she's been on the river and had a terrible fright."

Mrs Dimmock wailed and sighed, and someone brought her a tot of brandy. After she had downed it, she said in a croak, "Oh, what a thing to happen to a woman! Oh, it will be the end of me!"

"But can you tell us what happened?" Mrs Bailey the housekeeper asked, not for the first time.

"Oh … woe!" Mrs Dimmock struggled into a sitting position. "I was on a ferryboat crossing the Thames when the boatman was struck blind – just like that!" She snapped her fingers and reached for another tot of the brandy. "He let go of his oars and gave a great shout, saying he could no longer see the river in front of him."

The servants exchanged glances of horror. Abby, who was holding Grace, took several steps back.

Mrs Dimmock fanned herself. "The boat started to drift downstream towards the bridge," she said. "It looked set to crash into the pier, so one of the men on board grabbed the oar and paddled it along as best he could. Then … then the boatman gave a terrible roar of pain and fell into the bottom of the boat! No one wanted to touch him but when we got to Puddle Dock a ferryman came up and felt for his pulse – and, what d'you think? – he was stone dead!"

Everyone gasped.

"As dead as the old King!" Mrs Dimmock said. "And what's more, when they looked at him closely, he had the signs of the Plague in a ring around his neck! Red as roses, they were – and for sure, they weren't there when we set off!"

"But I expect you kept a good distance from him on the boat," Lizzie said.

"I did not!" Mrs Dimmock wailed. "Why, he took my hand to help me in and I sat right in front of him! Oh, for sure I have caught the Plague. I am a dead woman!"

"And we will be dead and lie in our graves beside you, unless you go from here and seek out a pest house!" Mrs Bailey said.

There were murmurs and nods from the servants, but a cry of horror from Mrs Dimmock. Pest houses contained the very lowest of the lice-ridden low. "You surely wouldn't make me go into one of those filth holes!" she sobbed.

"Rather *that* than let you infect every last one of us," another servant said.

Mrs Dimmock fell a-weeping then and begged everyone to spare her from the horrors of the pest house. She sobbed so very pitifully that Mrs Bailey (who had long been her friend) said at last that she could send a message to her mother to ask to be taken in. While Mrs Dimmock waited to hear her mother's answer, she would have to stay locked in the boot room outside, eat all her meals there and sleep on a straw mattress.

The next day, Mrs Bailey gave the maids at Belle Vue House posies of herbs to sniff when they went into the streets, and good luck charms to keep in their pockets.

"Breathe through the herbs at all times," Mrs Bailey told them. "Stay out of crowds, don't pet any stray cats in case they carry the sickness and hold this in your hand if you go near an infected area." *This* was the word 'ABRACADABRA', written in the form of a triangle on a piece of card. It was said to protect anyone who carried it.

A day later, Abby made her way to Hannah's shop, with a posy of herbs in her hand and the charm in her pocket.

The shop was a clean and sweet-smelling place, with a painted sign of a sugared plum. There were wooden shutters outside which came down to make a counter for serving.

Hannah greeted Abby with a smile, but she looked rather embarrassed. "Abby, I'm so sorry I haven't called on you!"

"I was worried in case you ..." Abby began, and then smiled, "but you look very well indeed."

"We've been busy making sweetmeats to prevent Plague," Hannah said. She pointed to a poster on the wall with a list of herbal sweets.

"*Do* they prevent it?" Abby asked. She sniffed at the posy she held. "Any more than these pretty herbs do?"

"Who knows?" Hannah shrugged. "They can't do any harm." She waited until there was no one else in the shop and whispered, "We have just heard – 3,500 dead in the last week alone!"

Abby gasped.

"And they have dug five new plague pits," Hannah added. "Truly, we would leave London if we could, but it is impossible for anyone but the very rich to get travel warrants."

"But would you really leave?" Abby asked.

"In an instant," Hannah said.

"What if you had a baby who relied on you for everything?"

"Ah," Hannah said. She looked at Abby with pity. "So your mistress is still not better?"

Abby shook her head. "I wondered if you might have something to tempt her appetite."

Hannah looked at the sweetmeats in the window, laid out in lines on their white trays. "Alas, we have no frosted rose petals or anything dainty – but they say sugared angelica is good for the stomach."

"Then I'll take some," Abby said. She lowered her voice. "For I fear she is failing fast."

The following afternoon, Abby was washing clothes at the sink when she heard a scream, and Lizzie came running in the back door.

" 'Tis Mrs Dimmock!" she said, before Abby could ask. "On the floor of the boot room – stiff as an admiral's hat."

"Never!" Abby cried.

"True as I stand here," Lizzie said. "I was going to leave her some bread and cheese, and I looked in through the little window and there she was, lying flat out with her eyes wide open."

No one was willing to move Mrs Dimmock – no one so much as wanted to *touch* Mrs Dimmock. Since it could not be kept a secret any longer, Mrs Bailey informed Mr and Mrs Beauchurch of the death of their cook (she was careful not to say anything about Mrs Dimmock's journey on the ferry). Mr Beauchurch sent a message to the authorities to send the death cart round, but he was not as concerned as he might once have been. For he was bothered by a mighty headache and had pains in all his limbs.

# CHAPTER 9

The third week of August, 1665

Abby took the baby into the yard to keep her out of the way. Toby was there stuffing things into a canvas bag. She stared at him. "What are you doing?"

"Getting ready to leave London!" he said. "We have to go now. We can't wait for a dark moon – or even for night-time."

"But –" Abby began.

"The Searchers of the Dead are coming," Toby cried. "If they say that Mrs Dimmock had the Plague, then they'll order the house to be closed and we'll all be trapped. It will mean death for the rest of us."

Abby's heart dropped. "Then ... then you're determined to leave?" she asked.

"If we don't, Abby, we're going to die," Toby told her. "Come with us!"

"But how can I?" Abby was silent for a moment as she looked down at the baby in her arms. "Unless Grace could come too."

But Toby shook his head. "We'll be travelling across country and sleeping rough. A baby wouldn't survive. Besides, they would say it was kidnap. You'll have to leave her here."

"But she's precious. Who would care for her?" Abby asked, her heart breaking.

Toby shrugged. "A new nursemaid."

"Really?" Abby said through her tears. "Do you think so? Where would you find a nursemaid willing to work in a house which had a red cross on the door?"

Toby shrugged again – he didn't know.

"I'll come with you, Toby!" Abby turned to see that Lizzie had come into the yard behind them. "I'm not going to stay here and rot," Lizzie declared.

Toby hesitated. "All right," he said at last, "but we're leaving right now."

Lizzie ran in to get her things, while Abby looked at Toby. She'd thought he cared for her – and perhaps he did. But not enough to stay with her in a shut-up plague house.

"Will you do one thing for me?" she asked.

"Of course. If I can."

"Will you go to my friend Hannah's sweetmeat shop in Crown and King Place, and tell her what's happened? Say that if she comes round and calls up to the nursery window, I'll come and speak to her."

"I will. And Abby ... I'm so sorry you can't come with us." He took her hand and kissed it, and she managed the smallest of smiles before she turned away.

Abby watched as Toby, James and Lizzie slipped out of the open back gate. She hid her face in Grace's soft shawl so that they wouldn't see she was weeping.

The Searchers of the Dead came to the house. When Abby saw these horrid crones approach, she took Grace to the nursery and stayed there, out of the way, until they'd gone. She noticed that her hands were trembling when she picked up Grace and fretted at the change she felt in herself. She'd believed that she was safe from the Plague, but now its dark shadow seemed to be stalking her.

The Searchers examined Mrs Dimmock's body and confirmed her death was due to Plague. No one had expected it would be anything else.

It was arranged that the death cart would call, and one of the Searchers wrapped Mrs Dimmock's body in a winding sheet to leave on the front step. She pocketed Mrs Dimmock's gold wedding ring as she did so. Builders came to board up the house. As Abby heard the planks being nailed across the downstairs windows, she shivered in dread.

***

Several days went by. Loutish guards stood at the front and back doors to check that no one went in or out of the house. These guards were willing, for a silver sixpence, to deliver messages or go to the market for food. But most of the food that was ordered never arrived, and many a sixpence went into a guard's pocket without the message reaching its destination.

Abby found it tiresome in the extreme to be imprisoned in the house. She couldn't even walk around the yard – no one was allowed out there for fear they would try and escape over the wall and spread the sickness further.

Details were taken of the three servants who'd escaped, but everyone knew that there was very little chance they'd be caught. A bad-tempered parish nurse arrived to look after Mr Beauchurch, who still had crippling pain in his head and arms. But the nurse did very little nursing. What she did instead was go through the contents of the kitchen cupboards and pass anything worth selling to her relatives outside.

In the days that followed, the nurse came more and more often to the house. As well as Mr Beauchurch, Mrs Bailey and one of the maids had now also been taken ill. By then, the nurse had seen the finery of the upstairs rooms, and she was biding her time until she could get her hands on the treasures there.

Mrs Bailey died, and another maid took ill, but Abby remained in good health. She took care of the baby, played with her, fed her and kept her safe, and did not dare to think about what the next day might bring.

# CHAPTER 10

THE FOURTH WEEK OF AUGUST, 1665

Hannah heard that Belle Vue House was shut up, and went round to see Abby as soon as she could. The guards were still outside, front and back, but Hannah ignored them. She stood where they couldn't see her, under the nursery window, until Abby appeared.

"I'm so sorry I couldn't come before," Hannah said. "My sister and I have been busy making sweetmeats to ward off Plague."

"I fear any sweetmeats come too late for this house," Abby said dully.

"I heard about Mrs Dimmock ..."

"Mrs Bailey the housekeeper has died since – and a maid and one of the grooms who was living in the barn."

"No!" Hannah cried, shocked. She took a deep breath. "But maybe that will be all," she went on. "Maybe the sickness has taken everyone it wants in this house."

"No," Abby said. "I've thought that with every death. But last night Becky the maid was overcome by a great fever. She went to bed moaning and crying, her skin so hot to the touch that it almost burned. And today she hasn't stirred from her bed and I know if I go to her room I will find a corpse."

Hannah fell silent.

"That leaves just my master and mistress," Abby said. "And perhaps a groom in the barn. And me – and Grace, of course."

Hannah felt near to tears, but tried to hide this from her friend. "But you are doing well!" she said. "I have some fresh bread here for you, and some rosemary bonbons! Sarah and I made them specially."

"That's kind," said Abby, with a sigh.

"Shall I give them to the guard at the door?" Hannah asked.

Abby shook her head. "That lout keeps half of everything we are given. Wait – I'll let down the basket."

She disappeared for a moment and came back with a wicker basket on a rope, which she lowered to the ground. Hannah put in the food, blew her friend a kiss, and promised to return as soon as she could.

Two days later, Abby stood at the nursery window and rocked Grace in her arms. Abby had been worried that morning, thinking that the baby felt hot and might have a fever. But Grace had taken her milk with no trouble and was now fast asleep.

Abby looked down at the child. She was such a pretty and happy baby, and she would inherit so much – the great house and lands, rich jewels and costly goods. But all those things counted for nothing if the Plague came knocking at the nursery door.

Abby liked to stand by the window, for it gave both her and Grace a little fresh air. Not that there *was* much fresh air in London. The whole City suffered under the stench that came from each bursting graveyard, every shut-up house and overfilled plague pit.

What would happen, Abby wondered, if every last person inside the city walls died? Would London become a ghost town, a town of spectres and spirits? And then, like in the fairy tale, would some brave souls come in a hundred years' time and reclaim it from the ghosts?

"Abby!" A faint call broke into her daydream. The hand-bell Mrs Beauchurch kept to summon servants rang several times. Abby put Grace into her cradle and rushed along to her mistress's room.

Mrs Beauchurch was standing in the middle of the room, swaying. She was as white as the nightgown she wore, and she had a hand to her throat as if something was paining her.

"Madam!" Abby said in alarm. "What are you doing? You must take your rest."

"But I cannot rest on my husband's death bed!" Mrs Beauchurch pointed at the vast four-poster bed.

Abby looked. Mr Beauchurch was stretched out across the bed. His hands were as stiff as claws, his face screwed up, his eyes staring at the ceiling.

"I cannot lie beside a corpse!" Mrs Beauchurch sobbed.

Abby breathed deeply. "Of course not, Madam," she said, as calmly as she could. "Come away, and I'll make up a bed for you in another room."

Mrs Beauchurch shook her head, and it looked as if it pained her to do so. "I cannot spare the time," she said. "There is much I must do before I die."

"Die? But your health is improving, Madam," Abby lied, hoping to make her feel better.

"I fear it is not," Mrs Beauchurch said. "See! I have the swellings in my neck." She moved into the light and Abby saw with horror that there were two bulging lumps, one each side of her jaw. "I can hardly move my head for the pain of them," Mrs Beauchurch moaned.

Tears came into Abby's eyes. One death after another – there seemed to be no end to the horror. "I'll get the parish nurse – or send for an apothecary," she said.

" 'Tis too late, Abby," Mrs Beauchurch said. "Much too late. Listen. I have only one wish, and that is that my child should live and prosper."

Abby nodded. "Of course, Madam."

"You and I will never travel into the country together. But I want Grace to go!"

"But how ...?"

Mrs Beauchurch raised her hand. "Listen to what I am about to tell you," she said. "I fear I have not much longer on this Earth."

# CHAPTER 11

The Plague was no respecter of riches or power.
It carried off Mr Beauchurch just as easily as the
lowest of his servants. In Belle Vue House at the
beginning of September, only Mrs Beauchurch,
Abby and Grace remained alive.

As Abby stood by the nursery window,
looking out for endless hours, she sometimes
wondered if she should have left Grace and gone
away with the others. She thought of Toby,
wondered where he might be, and shed a few
tears. And then she saw the baby's eyes fixed on
hers, looking puzzled and anxious.

'Could a baby really look in such a way?' Abby
wondered. And so she forced a smile and began
another game of peek-a-boo.

When they were tired of games, Abby held Grace up to the window, gazed over the rooftops, and told the baby stories about London. She spoke of the King and his mistresses, about the marvellous Royal Exchange, the theatres, the river, the stalls selling hot dumplings and honey cakes and the music man with his dancing monkey. She told Grace about her mother and father, too, and how precious she was.

When Hannah came round again, Abby could see that she was shocked at the sight of her. Abby had let herself go, she knew that, but it hadn't seemed worth washing or putting on a clean shift when the only company in the house was a near-dead woman and a pack of rats. But now she saw how neat and tidy Hannah looked, she made an effort to run her fingers through her hair and brush crumbs from her gown.

Hannah asked her to lower the basket so that she could send up bread and cheese and a cold meat pie. "How are you?" she asked.

Abby shrugged and shook her head. "One of the guards told me that many more died this week – near 8,000."

"But do *you* keep healthy?" Hannah asked.

Abby nodded, though in fact she felt a little dizzy. This was probably due to lack of good food, she thought, or being shut up for days on end. She couldn't even let herself think there might be any other reason. She took out the food from the basket. "In return for the food, I have something for you," she said. She took out a letter from her pocket, put it in the basket and began to lower it.

"What is it?" Hannah asked. She seemed rather worried about taking something from a house where so many had died.

"A letter from Mrs Beauchurch offering you and your sister a chance of getting out of London."

Hannah's face lit up. "Do you really mean that?"

"It was going to be the way that she and I were going to escape," Abby said. "But I fear the poor woman can only have hours to live. If she is not already dead," she added, almost to herself.

"But *you* are well, Abby. You could go," Hannah said.

"The front and back doors to this house are watched day and night," Abby told her. "It would be impossible for me to escape. Besides, it needs two to go together."

Hannah looked puzzled at this. "But ... I grant it is very kind of her but ... How is it that your mistress wants to help me and Sarah?"

"What she wants is for you to take her child with you into Dorsetshire," Abby said.

"And how would this happen?"

Abby leaned against the window. She was still dizzy and there were pains down her legs, but she didn't want to say anything to Hannah in case she took fright and ran away.

"You and your sister must pretend to be Mrs Beauchurch and myself," she said. "That's who the travel warrants are made out for. When they stop you at the Gate, your sister must say that Grace is her child and that she's been too ill to travel until now."

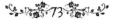

"And where will we get these warrants?" Hannah asked.

"They're all ready – signed by the Mayor himself. And there's a carriage and driver waiting at the Eagle and Child. It's explained in the letter!" Abby stared down at Hannah, begging her with her eyes to pick the letter up. "You must go home now and tell your sister about it. Beg her to go."

"I don't know if I should," Hannah said. "They say that nothing should be taken from an infected house."

"You can steam the letter over vinegar when you get in …" Abby said. "Oh Hannah, you must go! It's the only chance the baby will have."

Hannah drew a deep breath and, after another moment, she picked the letter out of the basket, blew Abby a kiss and disappeared.

Abby pulled up the empty basket. She remained at the window for a little while. Darkness was fast falling and there was little to be seen on the streets, only the death cart on its endless, weary round. Abby felt strange and light-headed. If she was going to get Plague, she

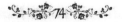

thought, then she hoped for a quick death, not painful and long-drawn-out. But oh, she didn't want to die! Not yet. Not until Grace was safe.

Abby walked along the hallway and stopped at the door of the room where Mrs Beauchurch had been sleeping. When she'd looked in on her before, her mistress had been struggling to breathe – her breath rasping and catching in her throat. Abby had heard it before. The death rattle, they called it. The last desperate effort to draw air into the lungs. But now all was quiet.

 CHAPTER 12

STILL THE FIRST WEEK OF SEPTEMBER, 1665

Abby drifted into a feverish sleep and was woken some time later by a scritch-scratch on the wooden floor. She opened her eyes and saw a grey rat, as big as a penny loaf, scuttling from one side of the room to the other. This was followed by another rat and then – was she still asleep and dreaming? – a whole line of them, each one close to the tail of the one in front.

The clock on St Martin's Church began to strike midnight and Abby sighed as her senses drifted. The chime of the bells mingled with other sounds – carriage wheels turning on cobbles and the cries of the watermen on the Thames. Abby felt as if she was floating above them. Her head hurt dreadfully and she wanted to go back to sleep.

But then there came different noises from outside – urgent calls, and another skittering sound. Not a rat this time, but a handful of gravel being thrown in the open window.

Abby managed to sit up on the bed. She looked over to Grace, who was still fast asleep, and then she moved to the window, trying to keep her head as still as possible. She knew she had something important to do but she felt strange and removed from the world. The pains in her head were so bad it felt as though someone was beating a club on her skull.

She looked out of the window to see Hannah in the shadows below the house.

"Oh, thank goodness!" Hannah said. "I've been standing here a half-hour or more. I thought you must be –"

"I fell asleep while I was waiting for you," Abby said.

"I had to talk Sarah into coming here," Hannah said. "She was worried about taking anything from the house in case ... you know."

Abby nodded. She *did* know that there was some danger ... something evil lurking not far away, but she couldn't quite remember what it was.

"Mrs Beauchurch explained everything in the letter," Hannah said. "Sarah's waiting around the corner in the carriage which will take us to Dorsetshire."

Abby gave a slight nod.

"Are you all right?" Hannah called up. "I can't see you. Can you light a candle?"

A candle. Abby knew there was a tinderbox and candle on the shelf in the nursery. She steadied herself and looked around. But the room was spinning and she couldn't think where the shelf was.

"Abby!" Hannah called in a loud whisper. "Did you hear me? Can you light a candle?"

Abby tried to focus. She found the shelf and tinderbox, made a spark and, after a moment, she managed to light the candle. It flared up, and its pale glow reflected her face in a little mirror on the shelf.

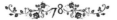

She glanced in it then gasped, shocked. "There … there's a girl here," she stuttered.

"A girl?" Hannah's puzzled voice came from below.

"In the mirror."

"It's just your reflection, Abby."

Abby turned her head this way and that in front of the mirror. "Ah, see! It is me, but I've been gifted."

"What are you talking about?" Hannah asked. Another moment went by. "*Abby?*" she called, louder this time.

Abby went on staring into the mirror. "I have the roses around my neck," she said, and her voice sounded very matter-of-fact. "I've been waiting and waiting for them."

Hannah's voice lifted in horror. "You have –"

"Yes. I thought, in the end, they would come."

There was a long, long silence and then Hannah said in a determined voice, "I'm going to take the baby, Abby. My sister and I – we are going to take Grace out of the city to where she'll be safe. Do you remember?"

"Perhaps ..." Abby wasn't sure if she did remember.

"You do love the baby, don't you?" Hannah asked her.

"Yes! Oh yes," Abby said, with something like a sob in her voice.

"Then together we must get Grace out past the guards." Hannah paused, then added, "You must pass her down quite naked – she mustn't bring a stitch of clothing with her in case it's infected."

"*Infected* ..." Abby repeated. She was no longer sure what the word meant.

"Abby, I want you to undress Grace, then put her in the basket," Hannah said. "You must make sure the rope is tied well and the knot is true."

Abby started to weep.

"Remember you told Mrs Beauchurch that you would love Grace as well as her own mother?" Hannah's voice was desperate.

"Yes," Abby whispered.

"*This* is what a mother would do," Hannah said. "She would give up her child so that she might live. You must kiss Grace goodbye and let her go."

Abby touched her fingers on the places around her neck where the blotches bloomed pink against her pale skin. "I must not kiss her!"

"Then be brave, Abby. Let her come now."

Abby's cheeks streamed with tears as she undressed the baby, settled her in the basket and took her to the window. She whispered a prayer, then began to lower basket and baby to the ground.

Hannah waited in dread until the precious burden came within reach. Then she steadied the basket and reached in for Grace. She lifted her out and wrapped a shawl around her. "Abby," she called up, biting back tears, "I've got her safely."

There was no reply and she looked up to the window, but Abby had disappeared.

"*Abby?*" Hannah called. And then called again, a little louder.

There was no answer.

Inside Belle Vue House, the candle on the shelf flared once, then guttered and went out. A thin wisp of smoke drifted up, hung in the air a while, and then disappeared.

A rat scuttled somewhere out of sight. And then the house was silent.

A Note from the Author

This book is based on a real event. During the Great Plague, Samuel Pepys wrote this in his famous Diary:

'A saddler, who had buried all his children dead of Plague, did desire only to save the life of his remaining little child, and so prevailed to have it received stark naked into the arms of a friend.'

There is a painting in the Guildhall Art Gallery in London that shows a young child being lowered to the ground in a basket. (It was painted much later.)

The characters in this book are invented, but all the details and events are true. The Plague was a terrifying and mysterious disease, which was not understood, and people grabbed at any chance to save themselves. They tried all the strange things that appear in this book.

We believe that the Plague killed around a third of the population of London – more than 100,000 people. Most of these were poor people. They had no means of getting away from the city, and nowhere to go even if they managed it. No one in the surrounding towns and villages wanted Londoners, in case they brought the Plague with them.

'Pest houses' were built on the roads into some villages. New arrivals were forced to stay in them for 40 days to prove they were healthy before they were allowed to enter.

We estimate that over 4,000 dogs were killed in London alone, and perhaps 12,000 cats. This was because it was thought that they might be spreading the disease. If only they'd been left to run free, the Plague might not have spread as far and as fast as it did. It was only many years later that it became known that the Plague had been spread by rats. Rat fleas, carrying the Plague germs, had moved on to humans and infected them.

No one knows how or why Bubonic Plague died out, but it never hit Britain so hard again. When the warmer weather came the following year people feared that the sickness would return to London, but thankfully, it never did. However, there were smaller – and just as devastating – outbreaks in other parts of the country.

I have told more of Hannah's story in *At the Sign of the Sugared Plum*, and the story of what happened to little Grace, Hannah and her sister after they went from London in *Petals in the Ashes*.

Our books are tested
for children and young people by
children and young people.

Thanks to everyone who consulted on
a manuscript for their time and effort in
helping us to make our books better
for our readers.